PEMBROKE WELSH CORGIS

BY LIBBY WILSON

Apex is distributed by North Star Editions:
sales@northstareditions.com | 888-417-0195

Produced for Apex by Red Line Editorial.

Photographs ©: Shutterstock Images, cover, 1, 4–5, 6–7, 8, 9, 10–11, 13, 16–17, 18, 20, 20–21, 22–23, 24, 25, 26–27, 29; iStockphoto, 12; AP Images, 15

Library of Congress Control Number: 2023922216

ISBN
978-1-63738-911-9 (hardcover)
978-1-63738-951-5 (paperback)
979-8-89250-048-7 (ebook pdf)
979-8-89250-009-8 (hosted ebook)

Printed in the United States of America
Mankato, MN
082024

NOTE TO PARENTS AND EDUCATORS

Apex books are designed to build literacy skills in striving readers. Exciting, high-interest content attracts and holds readers' attention. The text is carefully leveled to allow students to achieve success quickly. Additional features, such as bolded glossary words for difficult terms, help build comprehension.

TABLE OF CONTENTS

CHAPTER 1

FEARLESS HERDER

A Pembroke Welsh corgi races across a field. Her name is Beda. She is herding a bull into a pen.

Farmers can use herding dogs to move animals to barns or fields.

Corgis may herd by chasing, nipping, or barking at animals.

The bull lowers his head and **charges** at Beda. She rushes forward and nips his nose. The bull turns and runs the other way.

FAST FACT

Corgis can herd many animals. These include sheep, goats, and horses.

Bulls can be quick to attack. Herding dogs must move fast and be careful.

Beda keeps the bull running by nipping his back heel. He kicks his leg at her, but she dodges sideways. The kick misses. Then she chases him into the pen.

COMMANDS

Herding dogs learn many commands. Farmers use words, whistles, and hand signals. They tell their dogs which way to move animals. They also tell their dogs how fast to go.

The command "come-bye" tells dogs to move to the left of the animals.

CHAPTER 2

FARM DOGS

Corgis come from Wales. By the 1100s, many farmers owned them. The dogs herded ducks, geese, and cows. Corgis also guarded farms.

Corgis watch over people and animals. They make good guard dogs.

Pembrokes came from the Welsh county of Pembrokeshire.

There are two types of corgis. In the past, people sometimes bred the dogs together. But by the 1900s, they were separate **breeds**. Pembroke Welsh corgis are smaller. Cardigan Welsh corgis have longer tails.

FAST FACT

Welsh legends say corgis were bred by wood fairies. The fairies rode them like horses.

Cardigans came from the Welsh county of Cardiganshire.

Pembrokes also spread to other countries. Some worked as farm dogs. But many became pets. People liked their friendly **personality**.

ROYAL DOGS

Queen Elizabeth II of England loved corgis. She owned more than 30 corgis throughout her life. The dogs lived with her at Buckingham Palace.

Elizabeth (right) became queen at age 25. She got her first corgi when she was seven. ▶

CHAPTER 3

PEMBROKE TRAITS

Pembrokes have long bodies and short, stubby legs. The dogs stand 10 to 12 inches (25 to 30 cm) tall. But they can weigh up to 30 pounds (14 kg).

Despite their short legs, corgis can run very fast.

Corgis have fox-like heads. Their noses are long. And their large, pointed ears stick up. Corgis also have thick fur.

CORGI COATS

A corgi's coat has two layers. The top layer of fur is **coarse**. The undercoat is short and soft. Having thick fur helps corgis stay warm. Their fur also blocks water.

Pembrokes have thinner faces than Cardigans. Pembrokes look more fox-like.

Fawn-colored fur
is tan or light red.

Pembrokes come in several colors. Red and fawn are two examples. The dogs can also be black and tan. Some corgis have sable coats. Their fur has black tips.

Sable coloring is the least common coat color for Pembrokes.

CHAPTER 4

CORGi CARE

Pembroke Welsh corgis are active dogs. They need at least an hour of exercise each day. They may bark, dig, or chew if bored.

Owners can go on jogs to help their corgis get exercise.

Owners can train corgis to be gentle with small children.

Corgis were bred to herd. They may nip children or other pets. Owners can teach corgis good **behavior**. Owners should start when their dogs are young.

WATCH THEIR BACKS

Corgis can hurt their backs if they jump from high places. Using steps or ramps can help. Owners should also be careful not to feed their dogs too much. Extra weight puts **stress** on corgis' backs.

Corgis may have trouble climbing onto or off of furniture because of their short legs.

Corgis are bold and smart. They learn quickly. So, many owners train corgis to do dog sports. **Agility** events are one example.

FAST FACT

Some corgis do Treibball. In this sport, dogs herd large balls into a goal.

In agility events, dogs run through courses as fast as possible.

COMPREHENSION *QUESTIONS*

Write your answers on a separate piece of paper.

1. Write a few sentences explaining the main ideas of Chapter 2.

2. Would you like to own a corgi? Why or why not?

3. How many layers of fur does a Pembroke Welsh corgi have?

    A. one

    B. two

    C. three

4. When might a corgi dig holes in its owner's yard?

    A. if the dog is left alone all day

    B. if the dog is playing with its owner

    C. if the dog wants to sleep

5. What does **dodges** mean in this book?

*He kicks his leg at her, but she **dodges** sideways. The kick misses.*

   A. barks loudly

   B. moves out of the way

   C. digs in the dirt

6. What does **separate** mean in this book?

*In the past, people sometimes bred the dogs together. But by the 1900s, they were **separate** breeds.*

   A. weak

   B. fast

   C. different

Answer key on page 32.

GLOSSARY

agility
A sport where dogs run through an obstacle course.

behavior
A way of acting.

breeds
Specific types of dogs that have their own looks and abilities.

charges
Runs at something, often to attack.

coarse
Rough or scratchy-feeling.

legends
Famous stories, often based on facts but not always completely true.

personality
The way a person or animal usually acts.

stress
Strain or pressure, especially types that cause harm or pain.

BOOKS

Davidson, B. Keith. *Herding Dog*. New York: Crabtree Publishing Company, 2022.

Nichols, Rhonda E. *Pembroke Welsh Corgis*. Minneapolis: Kaleidoscope, 2022.

Pearson, Marie. *Herding Dogs*. Mendota Heights, MN: Apex Editions, 2023.

ONLINE RESOURCES

Visit **www.apexeditions.com** to find links and resources related to this title.

ABOUT THE AUTHOR

Libby Wilson has loved books and reading her entire life. She enjoys researching and finding interesting facts to share with readers. Her favorite topics are nature, history, and inspirational people. For the past 11 years, Ms. Wilson has been owned by Molly, the world's sweetest golden retriever.

INDEX

ANSWER KEY:
1. Answers will vary; 2. Answers will vary; 3. B; 4. A; 5. B; 6. C